Y0-BRZ-294

THE COMPLETE
BOOK OF KONG

William Trowbridge

MAC
811.54
T863c

THE COMPLETE BOOK OF KONG

William Trowbridge

Missouri Center
for the Book

಄಄಄

Missouri Authors
Collection

Southeast Missouri State University Press

©2003 by William Trowbridge

Southeast Missouri State University Press
One University Plaza
Cape Girardeau, MO 63701

All Rights Reserved
First Edition 2003
Printed in the United States of America
ISBN: 09724304-4-X, Hardcover
ISBN: 09724304-5-8, Softcover

Acknowledgements

Thanks are due to the following periodicals and presses in whose pages these poems first appeared:

Another Chicago Magazine—"Kong Meets Godzilla," "September Kong."

Controlled Burn—"Kong Looks Up What He Takes To Be His Nickname."

The Florida Review—"Kong Gets an Audience with the Pope."

Green Mountain Review—"Class Clown."

Hiram Poetry Review—"Kong Turns Critic."

The Laurel Review—"Kong Looks Back on His Tryout with the Bears," "Outgunned atop the Empire State Building, Kong Consents to Mambo Lessons" (published under a slightly different title), "Kong Encounters Marlin Perkins."

Light—"Kong Becomes Old News."

Light Year—"Kong Incognito," "Viet Kong."

The Louisville Review—"Video-Date-A-Kong."

New Letters—"Kong Bares His Soul Regarding Miss Tyrannasaura Regina."

Poet & Critic—"Kong Views an Experimental Art Film at the City Library" and a special chapbook issue entitled *The Book of Kong*, in which the following works appeared for the first time: "The Heavy Ape Who Goes with Me" (essay), "The Madness of Kong," "Kong Approaches the Great and Terrible Poet," "Kong Breaks a Leg at the William Morris Agency," "Kong Tries for a Mature Audience," "Kong Hits the Road with Dan-Dee Carnivals, Inc.," "Kong Picks Door Number Two," "Kong

Answers the Call for a Few Good Men," "Kong Settles Down."

River City—"Director Hoover Welcomes Kong into the Bureau."

River Styx—"Kong Discusses *King Kong III* over a Power Lunch," "Kong's Acceptance Speech," "King Kong in Hell."

Spoon River Poetry Review—"How Kong Fit through the Gates of Heaven," "Long Dong Kong."

Sundog—"Plummeting, Kong Gets the Picture," "Mardi Gras Kong."

Tampa Review—"Kong Contemplates His Action Figure," "Kong Remembers Home."

The chapbook *The Book of Kong* is available in its downloadable ebook form from Smallmouth Press at its website: Smallmouthpress.com

Thanks also to:

The University of Arkansas Press for publishing "Baseball Been Not So Good to Kong" in my collection *Enter Dark Stranger* and for reprinting other Kong poems in that book and in my collection *O Paradise*.

The St. Louis Poetry Center for awarding "Kong Bares His Soul Regarding Miss Tyrannasaura Regina" the 2000 Stanley Hanks Memorial Poetry Award.

The Corporation of Yaddo, The MacDowell Colony, The Ragdale Foundation, and The Anderson Center, within whose facilities many of these poems were written.

Finally, special thanks to the following friends and colleagues for their encouragement and critical help: Paul Zimmer, Michael Martone, Robert Wallace, Jim Simmerman, Jonathan Holden, Miller Williams, David Citino, Bruce Bennett, Karla Kuban, and David Slater.

For Barry MacAnally
1941–1974
physician, artist, brother

Contents

Introduction

The Heavy Ape Who Goes with Me

Having heard the tear-thickened voice of confessional poetry drowned out by one of confessional prose, I've decided to give up my hitherto ironic detachment. I'm diving in. Here's my confession: My Kong poems have always embarrassed me. Unlike most of my other personae, Kong, to say the least, lacks high seriousness.

No, that's not it exactly. He's highly serious, but he tends to show it in rather crude ways. He is, of course, immense and graceless, habitually knocking over delicate objects — or simply stepping on them without even noticing. When angered, he does it on purpose. Furthermore, he's a compulsive failure, a creature either unable or unwilling to recognize his bestial nature. As X. J. Kennedy has noted, the historic Kong is an archetype, in the tradition of the pitiable beast. However, he seems to lack the poignancy of a Quasimodo or the metaphysical angst of a Frankenstein monster, neither of which character, as I recall, shares Kong's enthusiasm for panty sniffing. And, like Delmore Schwartz's Heavy Bear, my particular Kong drags me with him through all his stumblings and fumblings and graspings. Worst of all, people tend to like him. After my readings, he's the one they ask about — not my sensitive youth persona nor my witty philosopher nor my brooding teller-of-dark-truths. No, it's that damn ape, who may have more in common with the Whoopee Cushion or the Joy Buzzer than with organic form or the deep image. But there's something worse than what I said was worst of all: I like him, too. There. I've said it, and I think I'm glad.

And I have reasons, which I often think are sound. With exceptions such as the work of Albert Goldbarth, Paul Zimmer, Stephen Dobyns, Denise Duhamel, Billy Collins, Charles Harper Webb, Heather Ross Miller, and Ron Koertge, most of the contemporary poetry I read seems dismayingly humorless. Much of it is wonderful, sometimes brilliant, but even its joy often seems overly earnest, devoid of the sense of our shaky perch between nobility and buffoonery. Thus, its dominant voice may have drifted into yet another form of what Robert Penn Warren has called "pure poetry"—that which excludes "ugly words and ugly phrases . . . cleverness, irony, realism—all things which call us back to the world of prose and imperfection." To Warren's list I would add humor, sometimes of the crude sort—the fart in the Longinian high church. Certainly contemporary poetry hasn't shied away from the language and rhythms of prose, nor even from a kind of colloquial wit; but it has, by and large, kept well clear of the pratfall and the belly laugh, which are among our most potent defenses against the insanity and brutality of contemporary life. In the literature of recent decades, these defenses are found mainly in fiction, not poetry.

There. See? I even have something of an argument to justify my being tethered to the great ape. Yet, I, too, feel the counter-tug of today's great seriousness. I still wince when the "hungry beating brutish one" inadvertently knocks all my purer works off the lectern. Delmore, I know what you mean; honest to God, I do. But can't we lighten up a little? There's nothing wrong with a touch of the gross now and then. Sometimes it's even philosophically sound to be crude as hell—and it feels good, too, if you really think about it.

Proem

Kong Bares His Soul Regarding Miss Tyrannasaura Regina

OK, so we're not the perfect royal couple,
me a hermit and her temperamental
as a hot volcano and not what you'd call
"pretty." Standoffish, too, as if
warm blood and opposable thumbs were too
lowbrow for dining out on stegosaurus
guts. Maybe I could wear my hair
shorter, get a tail piece, learn to hiss
and bolt my food. Maybe then I'd find
the nerve to crush her boyfriend's spine
and ask her out.
        I should know better, but
those eyes, so green and deep you hardly
notice her head is two-thirds teeth
and her toenails lay down sets of foot-deep
divots.
        I don't know. Last night
I dreamed of someone lovelier: swept in
from the sea, golden-tufted like a bird of paradise,
who needed rescuing from pterodactyls
and teeny-weeny white men, and sang to Kong
in a voice so high it broke his heart.

I.

Kongs of Innocence

Kong Looks Back on His Tryout with the Bears

If it had worked out, I'd be on a train to Green Bay,
not crawling up this building with the Air Corps
on my ass. And it if weren't for love, I'd drop
this shrieking little bimbo sixty stories
and let them teach me to mambo and do imitations.
They tried me on the offensive line, told me
to take out the right cornerback for Nagurski.
Eager to please, I wadded up the whole secondary,
then stomped the line, then the bench and locker room,
then the east end of town, to the river.
But they were not pleased: they said I had to
learn my position, become a team player.
The great father Bear himself said that,
so I tried hard to know the right numbers
and how the arrows slanted toward the little o's.
But the o's and the wet grass and grunts
drowned out the count, and the tight little cheers
drew my arrow straight into the stands,
and the wives tasted like flowers and raw fish.
So I was put on waivers right after camp
and here I am, panty-sniffer, about to die a clown,
who once opened a hole you could drive Nebraska through.

Having Surrendered atop the Empire State Building, Kong Consents to Mambo Lessons

I never claimed to have natural rhythm,
despite my instructors' smug assumptions.
"Get hot, boy; get hep," they call
as I heave onto the pattern of tiny steps
and another partner sprawls screaming
beneath my one-two-and-turn.
This time they tell me to go on,
and I try, jerking and stepping
till my head throbs and their faces grow faint
and my feet . . . my feet begin to find the measures
as walls crack apart and window glass
scatters across the groaning floor.
One-two-and-then-turn; two-three-and-
then . . . they scramble for cover, shouting
"Break for lunch! Break for lunch!"
But I am now the rhythm and the melody,
tabasco-souled Latino, pelvic
with Perez Prado's "Patricia."
Coming through, you runty little bastards;
this mother's ape was born to dance!

Kong Breaks a Leg at the William Morris Agency

First this one: "Peetah, Peetah, Peetah!"
said up on my toes, taking tiny steps,
with lots of shoulder. Then, eyes fluttering,
"Ah have always depended on the kahndness
of stranghas." Finale with ruby slippers,
heels clicking, eyes vague. "There's no place
like home, there's no place like home, there's
no place like home." They said these wouldn't do:
too passé, not enough oom-pa-pa, that I
needed to butch it up a little, surprise them,
go for the blockbuster, the dynamite finish.
These words stung like bullets, but I told
myself to be a trouper, to break many legs.
"Imagine you're Pearl Harbor," I said inscrutably.

Kong Turns Critic

The man said, "He is a brilliant
special effect, given the film
technology of the Thirties, but
the story is hopelessly contrived,
even allowing for the strong mythic
element." The woman said, "No,
he looks too much like a stuffed toy,
a huge piece of period kitsch,
ludicrous when he tries for tragedy."
The man shook his hair and made smoke,
insisting, "Verisimilitude is irrelevant,
as in any Gothic melodrama." I marveled
at these mammoth words, wondering
how they were folded into such
little brains. I ate the man
first, then the woman, both stringy,
but then what's not these days.

Baseball Been Not So Good to Kong

Who could refuse to hear a little infield
chattering from men both American and nationalistic,
to be melted in a pot where even giants
are allowed to form a team without subjection
to arrest and firing squad, where Indians
play with pirates and the testiest reds
shake hands with Yankees. So I thought before
I learned of strike zones: in my case
eight by twenty-seven feet of naked
bullseye. And, worse, the bat: same size
required for giants as for blue jays,
hard to grip, the drag bunt impossible.
Even the giants claimed I mocked them
when I caught three bases with my hook
slide or struck the pitcher when the umpire
told me to. "BOOOO," they snarled, insulting
my nickname — giants maybe in their vicious
little minds. Pissants, if you ask me.

Kong Looks Up What He Takes To Be His Nickname

So, **monster:** "Any very large animal,
plant, or object." And more, after *adj*: "Gigantic,
huge, enormous," meaning that, when I'm next to
something small that utters words, each toe's
a monster, each eye, even my pointer, monstrous,
which explains this: "One who inspires horror
or disgust," likely why Fay so often
screams instead of talks, likely why
everybody does. Their smallness makes me
horrible. "Monster!" they shout and launch
the Dawn Patrol to pick me off, though
to the Latins, as distinct from the Dutch
and the Old French, the word means "Prodigy,"
which, in turn, to those same wise and no doubt
larger-than-usual people, means "marvel."

Kong Approaches the Great and Terrible Poet

I said I, too, was a dancer, a misfit
in love with the way these tiny trees
rave in spring and the slants of rain
moving in from fields. He told me
such lines were competent but nothing
compared to his "kettle you jabbered
as easily in the yard," and that only licensed
poets would get the joke in "the corner
of the wall his hat on" or the allusion
to his brokers, Flux and Entropy,
in "the earth had made him shrink
undeniably an oboe." He said
one can't be a true outcast without lines
like those. In short, I was petit bourgeois,
too wash-and-wear to bob for deep
apples or understand how the soul
is like a glass of milk spilled from a cracked
pitcher by a chiropodist about to think
of himself, though not absolutely
like that in every case. I went away
weak as a bush baby caught in sunlight,
knowing, from what I'd found in the land
of humans, that poets truly must be
its unacknowledged legislators.

Kong Encounters Marlin Perkins

I couldn't believe it. He said
it was "The Wild Kingdom," then pitched
a net over my instep. He was terrible
to look at, hair white as death
and a wrinkled grin beneath it,
and a sparrow's voice chirping
praise to "Mutu Omah," a mantra
perhaps or some household god.
Believing him their champion
come to avenge the little planes,
I tried to humor him. I smelled
no fear, and God knows I needed
the good will. So I flopped down,
rolled my eyes, bellowed panic,
presented my tender parts.
But nothing fazed him, grinning
and chattering at the little box
aimed at us by his retainer.
I thought, "This is some new tactic,"
but then he stopped, walked off
saying prairie chickens have to
prepare for a rainy day. That must
have meant something, but he just
left me lying there, clutching
my pointer. I'll be in millions of boxes
Tuesday night, after "Family Feud."
That was his boast. I'm afraid now,
and I miss the little planes.

Kong Picks Door Number Two

They hailed me in, this cult of refugees
from human form, intense as butterflies
half emerged from their cocoons: sprouting
rabbit ears, pepperoni, ailerons; swelling
proudly to tomatoes, hot dogs, catcher's mitts
to please a talking statue, whose teeth
outshined the altar lights. "Monty! Monty! Monty!"
they called, surging in. I backed away in awe,
crushing a carrot family, but he beckoned me.
"Monty! Monty! Monty!" I cried, cowed as they
brought me to the place of choice and revelation,
—love or shame behind each door, each curtain.
I shut my eyes, sniffed three times,
and caught a scent my pointer recognized.
"Door Number Two!" I blurted, to the fury
of the changing ones: tomatoes whirled, pizzas
hopped, angry chipmunks screamed, "No, no!
Curtain One!" "Door Three!" "Keep the lousy
hundred bucks!" But the great door opened
to reveal a big TV with La-Z-Boy recliner
and a woman dressed, I think, for mating.
Cheers swarmed like biplanes. "Am I human now?"
I asked, feeling bare and somewhat smaller.

Kong Answers the Call for a Few Good Men

He said if we girls thought we were men,
we had another think coming. I wished
to save my think for later, when everyone was free
to smoke them if he had them. Our task was called
"Greasing the Slopes," though the beach was flat,
and smooth as April moss. Anyone who couldn't
grease was called a "Yellow Faggot," whose grave
would require dancing on. I'd choose something
to go with how "Yellow Faggot" fluttered
my tongue and made me giggle almost as much
as when I sing "If You Don't Mind, Is That
the Chattanooga Choo-choo?" He said he wanted
to know who thought anything about this
was funny. He wondered if we had a comedian
in the bunch, who thought this was some kind
of faggot picnic. Then, raising his little
pointed stick, he asked if the comedian wanted
to take one step forward, to confer
with him man to man. This was our signal
to emerge from girlhood, so I raised my pointer
and tried a step that requires great risk
of self defeat and is called "Tour Jeté."
Afterwards a voice from beneath my heel peeped,
"Fall out! Fall out!" Reborn a man, I hoped
to have yet another think coming.

Kong Tries for a Mature Audience

The director told me I was a dusky prince
to fill the dreams of praying sisters,
who need much ritual before
they mate. They wear black robes,
even on their heads, and have secret
mating names. This one brought up moans
wide and deep as Mother's when the moon
swelled full. But I was not Kong. I played
"Friar Harry, the 'Pillar of Flame'
Whose Ashes Needed Nightly Hauling."
I strode to her in moonlight, bearing
a bouquet of oak trees and a bus.
This went well enough, but my pointer
would not stand. With all the lights
and all the helpers yelling, cheering,
"Come on, big boy," I felt no tenderness,
no heart to shape the long, dark answer
to her call. "Use the Method," he said.
"You are *fire*. Think of something that gets
you real hot." I recalled the sun
burning high and gold above my forest,
how the leaves sang to it each dawn,
how it touched my eyelids when I
raised my face to make the mountains
shudder with its name: the Light, the Light.
When I cried, the sister stopped,
sat up, lit a cigarette. I stepped back,
trying to say how love grows best on ferns
and moss. "Talk's cheap," she squeaked,
looking careworn and empty-handed.
So I tossed her the bouquet and the bus.

Mardi Gras Kong

At last I was in step, marching along,
blowing kisses while the band in front
played the theme from *Armageddon*. I fit in
with the regulars, with King Neptune
and the Plattsburg Marching Gators,
with Zulu and the Gay Pride Major-
ettes, with the leprechauns. I was normal
as Bruce Cabot; everybody was: America's
rainbow Slinkying up Canal Street.
Some days are for the larger hearts.

Viet Kong

Each one showed me his gold medal,
talismans from F-B-I, a name too holy
for them to say. These agents wished
to trade questions for answers, something like
the cult of *Jeopardy*. "Why do you spell it
with a 'K'?" they asked. I told them I knew
the state capitals but I did not know
spelling. I asked if I could try another
category, perhaps state capitals. They said
they believed I was being smart,
which was taboo, that I could remain silent.
I take this Fbi to be a jealous god,
full of paradoxes and taboos, but perhaps
not so good on state capitals.

Kong Incognito

The secret is to blend in, choose neutral
colors in patterns that break up the silhouette,
and, in my case, slouch a little, avoid vertical
stripes, and wear dark glasses. Even when
everything else is right, the eyes can betray.
And the voice, keep it deep in the throat,
like this: "Eeeeeee," being careful to always
say average things. For instance, when greeted,
say, "I am fine. What are you?" or "Yes,
the weather today is free of cats and dogs.
My temperature is typical." When driving
in heavy traffic, say, "Up yours, motherfucker."
This is what average people say to one another
when a foreigner's not around and they don't
have to shoot him before asking any questions.

Director Hoover Welcomes Kong into the Bureau

"We cannot forget that an army of 200,000 persons who
will commit murder before they die roams America."
       — *J. Edgar Hoover to the Holy Name Society*, 1936

He said though I looked a little on the dark side
and my posture needed work, it was my brow
that finally got me in. "Nice and broad," he said.
"The snap-brim looks all wrong on pinheads."
After he presented mine and shook my finger,
he told me we have *many* enemies,
people everywhere who just don't like us.
"You're telling me," I said. He said we must
remind ourselves that they are Communists
and gangsters, and that the very worst,
the Communist gangster perverts, are saying
things about us, that we're not like other people,
that we don't like being men, that we're too fond
of silk and crinoline, and sometimes suffer
urges. "I know," I sobbed, remembering
the premier: the whisper of Fay's gown, the sting
of flash bulbs and reek of big cigars.
When he wobbled out from behind his desk
and let me see, I stood up straight and swore
to keep the secret of the men who fight for womanhood
and wear high heels. I'd be a G-Man, a *ladies'* man.

Long Dong Kong

I told the police it wasn't that: it was a big
banana fritter Mother taught me how to make.
The secret's in how you mix the spices. I was
trying to name the franchise, and I loved the accents
on that low vowel rhyme, like three big bells,
swinging and donging, one behind the other.

They said they didn't want to hear any more
about swinging dongs and big bells, that I
was in enough trouble already, that they weren't
born yesterday. I said I wasn't either,
that maybe that made us like a family,
like a franchise. Joyfully, I picked them up
and hugged them till they looked like pressed
carnations. "How does Long Dong Kong
& Kin sound?" I asked. "Do I hear music?"

Kong Views an Experimental Art Film at the City Library

I sat behind the man in the motorcycle pants
and the woman with hair like a shocked sombrero.
All of us would be blown away in the vast concussion
of Tony's art, which was good. So said the leader,
a tube-shaped woman who made hand-washing
motions while recounting Tony's terrible struggle
to get where he was, which was by the cheese plate,
and apologized about the projector's being unworthy
to receive such a large piece of art, though somehow
adjustments were made. And so commenced a mighty
flickering. "FEED ME!" screamed a severed head
(Tony's). "CLOTHE ME! There is still all this, like,
SHIT GOING ON!" Much activity followed: a naked man
stood there, another looked aside, another
scratched his beard (all Tony, but with different
earrings each time). Finally, window curtains parted
to reveal a mushroom cloud, then Tony weeping,
then the mushroom cloud again. After applause,
the lights came on, and Tony himself stood
to tell us what to think, though he didn't think
anyone could say anything about what his pictures
meant. "Like meaning," he said, "always means
the same thing anyway: Bourgeois Capitalism
and Phallocentricity," which I'm almost sure
was the name of that Haitian-Irish tumbling act
I followed at the Orpheum. Finally, the man
in the pants asked Tony if he didn't think
that the treatment of artists was like the Holocaust
and where did he buy his boots, to which Tony
replied that questions about art were fascist and Gucci's
basement. Before leaving, I tried to drink
some carrot juice out of the little plastic cup.

Kong Hits the Road with Dan-Dee Carnivals, Inc.

Perhaps I was meant to travel with my kind
by caravan to Tupelo, Grand Forks, Danville,
to often say like the famous tenors, "Make it
one for my baby and one more for the road"
and other beautifully sad conclusions. I love
the dwarves and pinheads best. Ramon,
whose shoulders bunch like a vulture's
above his crooked legs, shares his Wild Turkey
with me by the funhouse after closing time. He
and I and Princess Bianca, with the sleepy eyes
and the skull peaked like a teardrop, talk
and laugh beneath the wide, indifferent tent
of night. Sometimes I perch them on my shoulders,
Bianca on the left and Ramon on the right and we
harmonize, swooning trees with the old songs
about the tenderness of lips in small hotels.
Ramon says no one but the badly formed,
the set aside, can remember all their lives
how to love. "Only death can make us forget,"
he says, "and that's why the rubes come to stare
and why they walk away nervous,
checking their purses and wallets for signs
of tampering." Then Bianca, gazing toward dawn,
will tell Ramon he's full of dwarf shit again,
up to his little moustache. Bianca says you either
claim some turf or you don't, that even a putz
like Vaughn Monroe could make you feel you never
heard "Dancing in the Dark" till *he* sang it.
Kong, too, is full of dwarf shit, but he means
to wail, like Bianca and the great putz Monroe.

II.

Kongs of Experience

Video-Date-A-Kong

Hi.

My name is King Kong. I once starred
in an awfully romantic movie, also called
King Kong, in which I suffered for my love
of beauty by being turned into a barn door
anyone could hit. At the end,
Robert Armstrong said, "'Twas beauty killed
the beast," and Fay Wray stopped screaming
and went off with Bruce Cabot,
which I found paradoxical. I didn't know
the half of it then. You can smoke that one.

As you can see, I wasn't really dead.
Neither was Bruce Cabot. This is called
"acting." It was supposed to provide
people in the Depression a reason to live.
Today this reason is called "Prozac."

I have had many jobs since my stardom. Maybe
you've seen the Kong masks or the electric
vibrating objects or the Technicolor
Kong movie. People make such things
without even telling me. This is called
"endorsements." I'm presently looking
for something with more of a future,
like being a poet or a ballroom dancer.

I feel somewhat strange, sitting
on this tiny chair while always remembering
to look straight into the camera. These lights
are very strong. My underarms have often
been more confident. It's hard to think
of any other appealing things to say.

Believe it or not, I'm 70 years old.

Quit college. The Depression and all.

38

"Name a few of your favorite TV shows,
sports, or movies. Try to use positive
body language. . ."

No, I haven't had time to discover
these names, especially since I accidentally
crushed Peoria in 1956.
Unlike the people of New York,
the people of Peoria don't forget easily.

Remembering to look relaxed but sincere,
what interesting hobbies do I have? Dancing.
I love to do the light steps. Call me Mr. Soft Shoe,
except in Peoria, which I already told you about.

In case you wondered, I'm not wearing
a costume. If I could take this off,
I would. It makes people run away
screaming. My ears ring all the time.

And some people come running back
with guns. It's a shit deal, believe me,
but, of course, my luck will change soon.
This is known as "the odds," which in my case,
have become much better than even, I think.

Though I'm not getting any younger.

I can figuratively say that a second time.

Boy!

Yep.

Boy.

Did I tell you I was 70?

Kong Remembers Home

Bali Hai it wasn't. Where do you take
a human sacrifice from Yonkers
to make a good impression? The jungle?
The magma fields? No, just back to the cave
for swamp water and brontosaurus tail—
not my idea of romance in the tropics,
but I had obligations, a contract
with that dance troupe behind the wall
I had to build. Maybe you thought
they built it, who couldn't thatch
a roof straight? You saw them in their
monkey masks and hula skirts? Pathetic.
Cross them, though, and you're plucking
little spears out of your ass for weeks.
And their sailor pals: when they snatched
Fay back, I should have sealed the door
for keeps and moved in with the giant sloth.

Kong Settles Down

They've locked me in with this lady gorilla,
Russian-bred, bulged up on steroids
till she's damn near big as me. Shot-putter,
they say. Couldn't pass the hormone test.
Face like a cypress root and conversation
to match. Can't even speak Russian. "Ooog!"
she says, and "Eyoop!" and "MMMMM!" those eyes
tidal with an oceanic lust. Is this it for me?
My piece of the famous Apple Pie? My pension
for fifty years of going for the It?
For being the only ape ever to master
the double take, the hundred-twenty-story
free climb, the half-gainer onto concrete?
"Give us your poor, your huddled masses," sure,
and we'll put them on exhibit at the Roxy.
A little peace, a modest portfolio, and,
for my old age, a cave in the Bahamas
or even Jersey City — was the dream too big?
Last night she bench-pressed me. Depressing.
But I have to give her this: when she wants to,
she can sway that seven tons of tush
smooth and light as a jungle waterfall.
And she wants to all the time. So, baby,
show me that walk and talk that talk;
we'll devour all the Pie and make apelets
who can chuck a shot from Kokomo to Minsk.

Kong Gets an Audience with the Pope

I said that, unless he minded, I wouldn't try
to kiss the ring, what with the chance
of sucking off his arm, but I did want
to say how much I liked the ceiling and how sorry
I was for smudging out God's finger
when I stood up and bumped my head. He smiled
and said the kiss was a formality and that God
can always use some touching up. When he asked
what church I went to, I told him I stopped going
because the drum ensemble gave me headaches
and I lost my heart to the latest sacrifice,
though her screaming in the cave didn't help
my head. As far as worship goes, I said,
I love how steam rises from the grates on 42nd,
the way it shifts with the breezes and lifts
into the sunrise. And there was this bald guy
who kept telling me to say "Hare Krishna"
and dance with him, which he was probably sorry
I tried to do. And then there's Fay, Kong's one
true faith, who'd like to see him chained
to a giant organ grinder.
                              "May she wed a Baptist
filing clerk," he sighed, and blessed my instep.

Kong Discusses King Kong III *over a Power Lunch*

He said he'd need 15 percent,
  and I said OK.

He said that included the revenues on the after-marketing,
  and I said OK.

And he said we'd have to do more with the anti-colonialism thing,
  and I said I could see that.

And we'd have to punch up the kinky sex thing,
  and I said, OK, I guess.

And the gory special effects,
  and I said, If we have to.

And the clothes-sniffing scene,
  and I said, Isn't that part of the kinky sex thing,

And he said maybe he should explain "kinky" to me,
  and I said maybe he should,

And he did,
  and I said, Shouldn't stuff like that go under "gory special effects,"

And he said, What kind of writer are you,
  and I said, a poet,

And he said he'd have his girl get in touch with my girl,
  and I said he could have his girl keep her paws to herself
  and flicked his kinky little ass over the lobster bisque.

Kong Contemplates His Action Figure

It doesn't even look like me,
with its coconut shape, its vampire teeth,
its great big ugly snarl. Wind it up
and it waddles and spits sparks. Sparking
Kong—call him Sparky, the plastic spook,
the woolly wind-up wog, just right
to give the kids a little scare,
the wife a giggle, the White Knights
another moving target. Is this
what they saw when I gave a hand
to stop that anaconda with its gut
full of commuters, to save Fay
from that flashing swarm of paparazzi
at the Orpheum? Is this the land
of big comebacks and BankAmericard,
of chili dogs and the great Babe Ruth?

You bet your monkey's uncle's lips it is,
and Sparky took strike one. But he'll
just scratch his nuts and point his bat
toward the upper deck in center.

The Kong

It's a bustin'-out dance
when new sensation is your game,
like if you washed your heart with lye
and wrapped your head in cellophane.

It's the Kong,
not the monkey or the swim;
it's called the Kong.
You got to be a little dim.

Like that guy in the Coasters
or a cootie or a flea,
you'll say Why
is everybody always pickin' on me.

You'll do the Kong,
not the boogaloo or pony,
gen-u-wine:
don't accept no phony.

You'll look a little funny
in a cargo net,
but don't start bitchin':
that's as good as it'll get.

Could be the Kong,
not the mashed potato;
get it on:
You know it ain't in Plato.

You're gonna see Manhattan,
with its savoir faire,
but you'll end up on your head
after Kongin' on thin air.

Blame the Kong;
scratch a lot and slap your chest.
I said the Kong,
not the waltz or minuet.

You'll be a better ape for it,
just you wait and see.
When you're a major movie star
and get rerun on TV,

thank the Kong,
not the pavane or tarantella,
yeah, the Kong.
You could dance it in the cella'

all night long;
don't need no song.
I could be wrong,
but I don't think so.

Kong Meets Godzilla

I was eating lunchware at the commissary
when he called me over to his table
and offered a seat. I felt this could be
a big step for me, though at first
he just sat there drumming his talons,
nursing a vat of Courvoisier. He said
he was trying to quit smoking
and flaming too. It was hard on his teeth
and made him constipated. He looked a lot
smaller than he does in films and in need
of a good night's sleep. He told me
that computer animation was going to
have us both pushing shopping carts
under the Harbor Freeway overpass
or, worse, doing those thirty-second spots
for Car City. The *real* thing's got no place
in Tinsel Town, he said, and besides, who
was afraid of us anymore with all
the hardware out there on the street. He said
he was going back to Japan, where there's still
a little respect for gigantic angry reptiles.
I told him I always wondered what kind
of reptile he was supposed to be. "Fuck you,
kapok boy," chirped a voice from behind
his chest. "No thank you," I said,
and moved back to my old window table.

Kong's Crush on Madonna

It was that steel
brassiere, leveled
at my heart. Cupid's
twin warheads,
heat seeking,
armor piercing.

Her eyes locked on.
She counted down.
I had ignition,
lift off.

The Madness of Kong

I think I see it now: they chase me
because I'm mad, and I'm mad because
they chase me. So said the doctor
when I told him I was kidnapped
from my secret island by movie men
and a tiny blonde in love with screaming,
that I was God and may still be,
that I'm immune to bombs and bullets.
He said it would be years before
I'm cured, that mother is behind it all.
When I pinched his head, it made
a little squeak. Sometimes it's good
to be mad, if you really think about it.

Kong Dines Out with His Many Friends

All right, fine: if you don't
have a chair, I want a big
table—and make it sturdy.
And for starters, bring me bananas.
See this hand? I want it full
of bananas. Anybody here think
there's something funny about me
eating bananas? Anybody think
it's good manners to sit
in a chair when someone else
has to sit on a table? ANYBODY?
That's better. Now, how about
a little entertainment? I like
dancing. Anything wrong
with liking dancing? Anybody
here not know how to dance?
Real fast? On the table,
flamenco style? FIVE, SIX,
SE-VEN, EIGHT. There you go,
and let's keep those arms up.
But I don't think I hear any "olés."
Kong gets sad when he doesn't
hear a lot of "olés."
                You know,
I almost forgot how good it feels
just to sit down and eat with friends.
Appetizer?

Kong Becomes Old News

I might as well be Bambi, though I stomp out
every morning, flattening cars, blowing raspberries.
On Wall Street, I pissed on a power breakfast.

Nothing. People plod along among the drive-bys
and weenie wavers, or this week's postal clerk
with an urge to downsize. The crowds won't scare.

I've spent whole weeks in my apartment, watching
trash-talk bouts and Viagra infomercials, or bulletins
from Headline News about more humans going ape.

I need a better agent, one with a downtown office,
whose contacts aren't all dead or in the home,
who'd get me off the list of fright-night hairies

and put me in a musical, where I could dust off
my tenor and my tap routines, be the Fred Astaire
of lovesick giant apes, lifting up my Ginger.

Plummeting, Kong Gets the Picture

I should have seen it sooner:
"Beauty and the *Beast*." The whole thing's
just to show I should have known
my place: cheap thrill for the locals
back in Nowheresville. Try
for a life on the pavement side
of the fence, a little class,
a little oo-la-la, maybe
some cheers instead of screams,
and I wind up temporary
detour for Beauty
and her drawling hunk,
then, after the next
ten floors or so,
jumbo grease spot
on the Great
White Way.

O world
of sticky fruits
and fanfares,
come to Papa!

Konganelle

For a leading man, I'm much too tall.
My lot's to stare down raptors, though
I see her eyes and, trembling, fall.

I've worked six months on waltzing small
while partners pop beneath my toes
like bubble wrap, more wide than tall.

Manhattan's where light feet are all
it takes to travel with the flow.
But I catch her scent and, stumbling, fall.

My life's a waiting for her call,
which sounds like hinges shrieking "No!
You're a hairy ape and much too tall."

They chained me in a vaudeville hall;
mobs shoved in to see the show:
a monster who, from grasping, falls.

My day grows short: the biplanes call,
a cleanup crew awaits below.
With riddled heart, and not so tall,
I touch her hair and, leaping, fall.

King Kong in Hell

"Sure, come on in," said Satan. "We're open
admissions, though we discourage applicants
who don't seek a quality type of torment,
a deep thrust towards excellence in perturbation.
We're customer-oriented here, a hands-on
system, participatory, with a maximum
of self-mutilation and hardly any of that old
passive sit-and-get-your-head-gnawed-on
routine. We use assessment so success
is never doubted. You'll feel the difference
right away: it's a kind of love." All right,
I thought, any kind at this point, to free
my heart from Fay, even if it burns
till blood steams out my ears, though such
love seems awfully like what the people
of New York already offer, and without the thrust
and big tuition. There's also Broadway, spotlights,
Gershwin and Berlin. "I'll take Manhattan,
the Bronx and Staten Island, too," I told him,
slipping on my top hat, reaching for my cane.

How Kong Fit through the Gates of Heaven

The sign was green, like on the interstate:
Welcome to Heaven: You've Died And Gone Here.
"The All-Knowing's latest," said the desk clerk, lifting
an eyebrow. He told me to take a number and go
sit with the other side-show types back
by the odd sizes bin, that the whole place
was closed temporarily due to overcrowding,
that they were going to put in a night shift
and add six cars to the Pentacost-O-Coaster
—and not to give him that tired crap about
the implications of "omnipotent" and "infinite,"
like those theologians did. They now sing warm-up
for the Gehenna Boys Choir, he said, though he doubted
a slack-jawed bag of monkey substitute like me
would catch his meaning.
                    "Could this be it?"
I asked, catching the little thing beneath his robe.

September Kong

Fay's kapok's going bad, settling
in low spots from cheek to thigh,
wrinkling her hide, sinking her eyes,
changing her prance to a vague
step taking. She won't scream anymore,
even when I slap my chest and do
my game face. She gets me mixed up
with Sylvester Stallone, says I shouldn't
wear my shorts so tight, should have
stopped with *Rocky II.* I don't look
so great myself these days, slothing
along the pavement, hair tufting thin
around my butt and forehead. Now
when the bullets hit, dust puffs
sprout like mushrooms on a month-old
carcass. What's it all about, anyway:
you're born a god, study the handbook,
learn all the knots and — whack —
you wind up bonus points on the merit badge
for sharpshooting. Then you start to sag
and leak. Should I call on my creator,
for the larger view, a little renovation —
the genius who did The Giant
Behemoth and Mr. Tooth Decay?
Maybe I'll take it up with Wardrobe.

Kong Discovers He's Immortal

So I guess that makes it me and Dracula,
that guy with the warthog breath and the joke
about being just his type. And everybody else
with a one-way ticket to the local Forest Lawn.
I'll bet De Mille's behind this, who reissued
the Commandments, did thirty-seven takes
of Cleopatra in the milk bath. Peeping Cecil
crouched behind his propane-burning bush.

So now? My agent says I ought to write
a diet book and hit the talk shows, but they'd
probably find out I don't eat. There's enough
to sweat without a lawsuit: what's retirement age
for the death impaired? Do I lose my 401,
my pension? Mother had it right: beware
of gift brides, especially when they're tied to stakes,
and buy no stock from Republicans in pith helmets.

Epilogue

Kong's Acceptance Speech

First, I'd like to thank
the little people

without whose swarming
I'd never have

squeezed through
the keyhole of Manhattan

or the needle's eye
called Broadway,

where I could have
wound up just

another face
in the screaming mob,

another guy
with a dream too heavy

to rise above
the parking meters.

And I'd especially like to
thank Robert Armstrong

for keeping this merchandise
moving and the lynch fever

epidemic. Of course I can't
forget Bruce Cabot,

whose conversation
made me sound

like a Harvard Ph.D.,
though I went to City College.

And finally, Fay,
who I'm told couldn't

be here tonight
due to a bad case

of laryngitis. She taught me
what real love is, how it can

make me want to stop
a belt of .50 caliber

just to catch a glimpse
of those ruby tonsils,

feel those pearly feet
tickling my lifeline.

Class Clown

First, here's a wonderful poem by Ronald Wallace:

Matheny

Remember me? The class jack-off.
In ninth grade I ripped up
a whole row of bolted-down school desks
and threw them out the music room window.
You applauded. You egged me on. I'd do
everything you wanted but wouldn't:
throb spitwads at the teacher,
snap any girl's bra strap,
blow farts on my naked arm.

M'weenie! you called out. *M'weenie!*

I took the heat, paid the piper, faced
the music, while you,
getting your rocks off, looked on.
Now who's the failure? You
with your teacup hands,
your bald smiles and small promotions?
Or me, Matheny, the flunky, the great
debunker. Your drab imagination's ingot.
The gold in your memory's coffer.

Most of us recognize Matheny, and we remember how he
thrilled and horrified us, the ones who got our rocks off
egging him on. The ones who followed most of the rules and
were rewarded with a college education and something that at
first seemed like what our parents called "a job with a future."
No one knows what happened to Matheny, whether he re-
formed and got what seemed like a job with a future, too, or
whether he kept resisting the enforcers and reformers and is
now dead or homeless or confined in some prison or mental
institution. All we know is that he never shows up at the

reunions—and that we're secretly glad he doesn't. It's not that we want him dead: it's just that we wouldn't know what to say to him and that, as the poem implies, we're a little afraid of what he'd say to us. After all, Matheny seemed to have no respect for much of anything, not even what we liked to think of as the finer things in life: the lettermen's club, cheerleading, Hi-Y, the authors' club, the National Honor Society, all of the achievements we wanted listed beneath our senior yearbook pictures. Here's what was under Matheny's name in the yearbook: "not pictured."

But was it just our cowardice that made Matheny so contemptuous of us? Maybe it was our treatment of him as someone beneath us, someone whose best use was to amuse us before we cast him off with the other childish things. Class clown: class bum. So Matheny got lumped in with characters like Big Foot Feron, the class bully, and Bernard Spoo, the guy sent to the state hospital for doing something unnamable to his little sister.

And, lo, when we got to college we learned, those of us who studied literature, that there are higher and lower types of writing as well as of people; that since people first wrote, the funny stuff was considered lower and the not-so-funny stuff higher. "Comedy," observes Aristotle in *The Poetics*, "is, as we have said, an imitation of characters of a lower type—not however in the full sense of the word 'bad,' the ludicrous being merely a subdivision of the ugly." Later thinkers went on to arrange all the known genres in a hierarchy, usually putting epic poetry at the top and, you guessed it, comedy toward the bottom. At the lowest level of all was satire, snotty comedy. We still seem to believe, at least when it comes to poetry, that comedy is vulgar, superficial, impure—the M'weenie in our homeroom—and, therefore, that the poetry we most admire should be humorless—all of this in spite of the convincing observation by Howard Nemerov and others that good poems and good jokes have a similar structure and dynamic.

To make matters worse, we may be clinging to the ancient notion that any mixing of humor and seriousness disturbs the natural order. Anybody who has a job with a future knows such tampering produces another of those spooky gene pools out of which has lurched numerous offspring of those vulgarians the modern fiction writers. But perhaps our urge for purity is more a matter of our need to feel that, despite all this country's fanfares for the common man, we're really aristocrats. Common man: common bum. With Sir Philip Sidney, and despite our American suspicions of decorum and its inviolable code of rules, we cringe a little at serious comedy or comic seriousness: "the commingling of kings and clowns," which results in the clown's "attempt to play a part in majestical matters with neither decency nor discretion. . . ." Chew that, Shakespeare.

But that's not all. Poems that produce laughs or at least smiles are often categorized as "light verse." Though the term wasn't originally meant to suggest something lightweight (If it had been, a lot of serious poems would have to be called "light verse."), people began to understand it in that way. And we still seem to — even when some of our major poets, Auden and Eliot, for instance, disagree. So humor is not only suspected of being a moral, social, and political pollutant, it's also denied the compensation allowed most other self-respecting anathemas: substance, heft, power. Satan got a better deal.

Matheny had a pretty clear inkling of our attitude toward his kind way back in grade school, not long after he applied cupped hand to armpit and discovered how we treated him after we got our rocks off. Deep down, we may actually dislike humor, especially when we catch it holding hands with our purse-lipped daughter Seriousness. It reminds us of embarrassing things about ourselves and our bloodline — about the red nose and slapstick hidden in the Edenic honeymoon suite. So we give Matheny the title of Class Jack-off, while the rest of us vie for Best Personality and Most Likely to Succeed. But we need Matheny, seriously need him to remind us that, even as we strike the heavenly lute of Sweet Poesy, we're not so highborn, so uncommon. And we seriously need him for at least another important reason, a glimpse of which the following excerpt from Peter Meinke's "The Gift of the Magi" provides:

> And Melchior told a story that
> had Joseph sighing in the hay
> while holy Mary rolled her eyes
> and Jesus smiling where He lay
> as if He understood, Lord,
> knew the joke was good.

But Balthazar began to weep
foreseeing all the scenes to come:
the Child upon a darker stage
the star, their spotlight, stuttering out —
then shook his head, smiled, and sang
louder than before.

There was no dignity that night:
the shepherds slapped their sheepish knees
and tasted too much of the grape
that solaces our sober earth.
O blessèd be our mirth, hey!
Blessèd be our mirth!

"Matheny" by Ronald Wallace in *Long For This World: New & Selected Poems* copyright 2003, reprinted by permission of University of Pittsburgh Press

From "The Gift of the Magi," by Peter Meinke, in *Liquid Paper: New & Selected Poems* copyright 1991, reprinted by permission of University of Pittsburgh Press